Sulamith Wülfing

The Little Mermaid

Text by Hans Christian Andersen

Sulamith Wülfing

The Little Mermaid

Text by Hans Christian Andersen

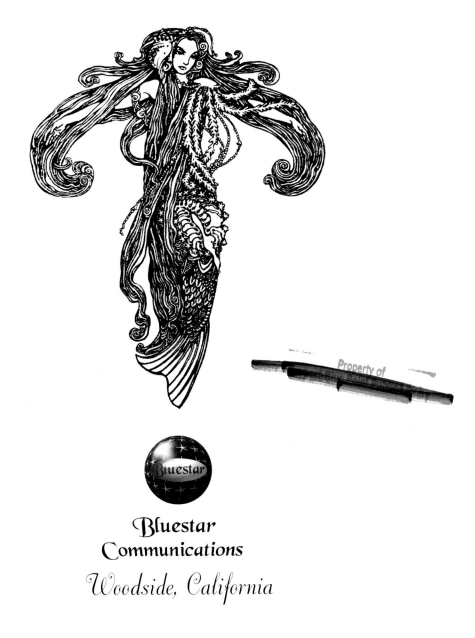

Bluestar
Communications
Woodside, California

Cataloging-in-Publication Data
Andersen, H. C. (Hans Christian), 1805-1875.
    [Lille havfrue. English]
    The little mermaid / text by Hans Christian Andersen :
[illustrated by] Sulamith Wülfing.
       p. cm.
    "Translated by Petra Michel. First published in German by Sulamith
Wülfing B.V. under the title Die kleine Seejungfrau"--Copr. p.
    Summary: A little sea princess, longing to become human, trades
her mermaid's tail for legs, hoping to win the love of a prince and
an immortal soul for herself.
    ISBN 1-885394-17-9
    [1. Fairy tales. 2. Mermaids--Fiction.] I. Wülfing, Sulamith,
1901- ill. II. Michel, Petra. III. Title.
PZ8.A542Lit 1997
[Fic]--dc20   96-21504
                                          CIP
                                             AC

Translated by Petra Michel
First published in German by
Sulamith Wülfing B.V. under the title
Die kleine Seejungfrau
Copyright © 1953 Sulamith Wülfing B.V.
This translation:
Copyright © 1997 Bluestar Communications
44 Bear Glenn
Woodside, CA. 94062
Tel: 800-6-BLUESTAR

Edited by Jude Berman
First Printing 1997
ISBN: 1-885394-17-9

Printed in Germany

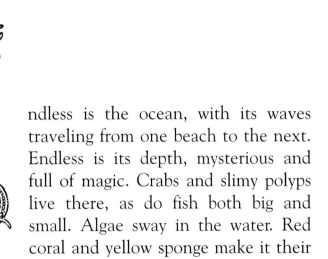

ndless is the ocean, with its waves traveling from one beach to the next. Endless is its depth, mysterious and full of magic. Crabs and slimy polyps live there, as do fish both big and small. Algae sway in the water. Red coral and yellow sponge make it their home. Down at the very bottom stands a magnificent palace, glittering with all the treasures of the sea. Its high windows are made of amber. Mother-of-pearl shells shine on its ceilings.

Once upon a time, the old Sea King lived in this palace with his six daughters. The youngest was the most beautiful. She had skin as delicate as rose petals and eyes as blue as the ocean. She was not like human children, however. In place of legs and feet, she had a fish's tail, as did her sisters. And she did not have a soul.

Her older sisters often spoke to her about the world of humans. They described big ships with white wings and lands with trees and fragrant flowers, birds that sing, and big houses built of gold and marble. They spoke about humans dressed in beautiful clothing who sailed these ships and walked along the beaches.

The little mermaid longed to leave the depths of the sea, as her sisters did. She longed to swim to the water's surface and visit this world. The more she heard about it, the stronger her longing grew.

But she had to wait. According to the laws of the sea, she was not allowed to see the sun or humans until she was fifteen

years old. Still, she longed with all her heart to love these human beings. Her longing would become so painful she needed to cry. But a mermaid cannot shed tears. Because she could not cry, she became even sadder.

Finally, she turned fifteen. The time had come for her longing to be fulfilled. She was beautifully adorned with pearls and coral, mother-of-pearl, and amber. Because she was the daughter of a king, eight magnificent oysters held tightly to the scales of her fish's tail. Then, as light and clear as a balloon, she emerged from the darkness of the deep sea.

The sun was just setting when her head appeared above the surface. The clouds, still tinted rose and gold, billowed like a city with huge palaces, walls, and bridges. The air was mild and fresh, and the sea calm. A lone star shone in the deep turquoise-blue sky.

For the first time, the little mermaid saw a ship with white wings. She heard music and singing. She saw colored lanterns and flags waving in the air. Red and green fires burned in large, iron pans. Hundreds of rockets shot into the air, spewing thousands of stars. Magnificent fire-fishes flew off the ship into the blue night.

The ship moved up and down with the rolling of the sea. Every time a swell lifted her, the little mermaid peeked through a porthole. Inside she saw crowds of men and women in festive dress. The handsomest of all was a young Prince with big, coal-black eyes. He could hardly have been more than sixteen years old. All the music, dancing, and candle light were to celebrate his birthday.

It grew late, but the little mermaid could not turn her eyes from the ship and the handsome Prince. Entranced by what she saw, she forgot about time and place. Deep down in the sea there was a rumbling. The waves grew mightier. Dark clouds gathered. Lightening flashed along the horizon. On the ship, the colored lanterns were put out, the music ceased, and no more rockets shot up.

The ship started to move. Sail after sail opened to the wind. But the bad weather had come too quickly. Waves, like mighty, black mountains, threatened to crush the mast. In one moment, the ship disappeared in the trough of the waves. The next moment, it was lifted to the top of a towering crest. Buffeted by the waves, its thick planks groaned and cracked. Water entered its portholes and its mast broke in two like a reed. The ship rolled so far to one side that water rushed into its hold.

The little mermaid saw that the Prince was in danger. If he drowned, he would go down to her father's palace dead. She had to help him! He must not die!

She swam among the drifting beams and planks, without a thought that they might crush her. She dove deep into the sea searching for the Prince. At last she reached him. He could no longer swim in the stormy ocean. His arms and legs had failed him and his beautiful

eyes were closing. He would have died if the little mermaid had not rescued him. She held his head above water and let the waves carry her wherever they pleased.

At dawn, the storm ended. The sun rose, bringing color and life back to the cheeks of the Prince. But his eyes remained closed, and no breath moved his lips. The mermaid stroked back his wet hair and kissed his high, noble brow. He was all hers. Her only wish was that he would live.

Before her was a land with glorious, green forests on its shoreline. Behind, snow-capped mountains lay like huge swans on the ground. Palm trees swayed gently with the morning breeze. The sea had formed a cove where the fine, white sand had washed up. Reflected in its calm waters, the mermaid saw the walls of one of those big buildings her sisters had described. She carefully laid the Prince, who was still unconscious, on the sandy beach. Then she swam further out, covering her hair and breasts with sea foam so that no one could catch sight of her. She waited for humans to find the Prince.

Bells rang out from the big building and a group of maidens came through the garden. The youngest ran joyfully toward the beach in search of amber and shells that might have washed ashore during the night. There, she found the Prince. At first she was frightened, but then she ran to gather her companions. Their voices awakened the Prince from his deep slumber.

The little mermaid saw him smile at the maidens with gratitude. He thought he owed his life to them. He did not smile at her, for he did not know it was she who had saved him. She felt very sad. After the maidens led him away, she dove sorrowfully into the depths of the water and returned to her father's palace.

The mermaid had always been quiet and withdrawn, but now she became even more so. Her sisters asked her what she had seen, but she would not tell them. Often, in the morning and evening, she would swim to the place where she had left the Prince. But she did not see him again, and returned sadder than before.

Finally, when she could endure it no longer, she confided in her sisters. One of them knew who the Prince was and where his kingdom lay. With their arms around each other's shoulders, the sisters swam through the waters to see his palace. It was built of pale yellow stone, with a great flight of marble steps leading down to the sea. Splendid golden cupolas rose above the roof. Marble statues that looked as if they were alive stood between the pillars.

Once she knew where the Prince lived, the mermaid often visited his kingdom. Hoping to gaze at her beloved, she swam much closer to land than any of her sisters had dared. Her long-

ing for the Prince and his world grew stronger. She became more and more fond of human beings and longed to live like them. She wanted to fly over the sea in ships, and climb the lofty mountains. She longed to know the lands whose fields and forests stretched further than her eyes could see.

One day, she decided to ask the dowager queen to tell her everything about human beings and the world above the sea. "If humans don't drown," she asked, "can they live forever? Don't they die, as we do down here in the depths of the sea?"

"Yes," replied the old lady, "they must die too. Their lifetime is even shorter than ours. We can live to be three hundred years old, but when we cease to exist, we are transformed into foam on the water. We have no immortal soul. We never have another life. We are like the green reed—once it is cut, it never grows again. Human beings, however, have a soul that lives forever. It lives after the body has turned to dust. It rises up through the air, up to the shining stars. Just as we rise out of the water and see the countries of the earth, humans rise to unknown beautiful regions that we will never be able to see."

"Why weren't we granted an immortal soul?" asked the mermaid in a melancholy voice. "I would gladly give the extra hundreds of years I can live to be a human being for one single day, and then go to that heavenly world."

"You must not think about that," said the old merlady. "We have a much happier and better life than the people up there."

"So I am fated to die and float like foam on the sea? I will not hear the music of the waves? I will not see the beautiful flowers and the red sun? Can I do nothing to win an immortal soul?"

"No, only if a human being were to hold you so dear that you were more to him than father and mother, if he were to love you with all his heart and join his hand with yours, promising eternal faithfulness—then his soul would pass into your body and you would share in the bliss of mankind. He would give a soul to you and retain his own as well. But that can never happen. The very thing that is considered beautiful here in the sea—your fish's tail—is considered ugly on earth. There, to be beautiful one needs to have two clumsy sticks, which they call 'legs.'"

The little mermaid sighed and looked sadly at her fish's tail. Nothing could make her happy—neither her sisters' games nor the magnificent court ball in her father's castle, where they

danced and played music. She thought constantly about the Prince. She could not forget her sorrow at not having an immortal soul.

While everybody else was joyful and gay, she stole out of her father's palace, and sat sadly in her garden. Suddenly she heard the sound of bugles through the water. She thought, He must be sailing—he whom I love and in whose hand I would gladly place the happiness of my life. I will risk everything to win him and an immortal soul! I shall go to the old Sea Witch who has always terrified me. Perhaps she can help me.

The little mermaid left her garden and swam toward the roaring whirlpools, beyond which lived the old Sea Witch. Before, she never would have gone near this barren place where no flowers or sea wheat grew. The water swirled around like a roaring mill wheel, sweeping everything down to the bottom of the fathomless sea. She had to pass through these whirling waters and across a warm, bubbling swamp to reach the house of the Sea Witch, who lived in the middle of a strange forest. All the trees and bushes were polyps—half animal, half plant. They looked like hundred-headed snakes growing out of the ground. Their branches were like long arms with slithery wormlike fingers that twined around anything they could grab from the sea.

Terror-stricken, the little mermaid stopped before the forest. Her heart beat fast with fear and she almost turned back. But then she thought of the Prince, and of a human soul. Her courage returned. She folded her arms closely around her breast and darted off like a fish. She swam among the hideous polyps as they stretched out their arms and fingers to catch her. She saw how each of them clung tightly to everything it had caught—humans who had perished at sea, ships' rudders, anchors, chests and planks, and even a little mermaid. That was the most horrible!

In the middle of the forest, in a big, muddy place, she found the Sea Witch's house. With her bloated, unshapely body, she was rocking in an empty snail shell and playing with sea snakes, toads, and other ugly creatures. She was not at all surprised when she saw the little mermaid.

"I know what you want," said the ugly witch. "It is foolish of you, and will only bring you trouble, my pretty princess, but all the same you shall have your way. You want to get rid of your fish's tail and have two stumps to walk with instead, so that the young Prince will fall in love with you and you will win him and an immortal soul!" She let out a loud and ghastly laugh. "You have come just in time. Had you waited until sunrise tomorrow, I could not have helped you for a whole year. I'm

going to brew a potion for you. Before the sun rises, you must swim to land with it, sit down on the shore, and drink it. Then your tail will disappear and shrink to what humans call 'pretty legs.' But it will hurt as though a sharp sword were cutting through you. Everybody who sees you will say you are the prettiest human they've ever seen. You will keep your gliding motion. No dancer will be able to move as gracefully as you. But at every step it will feel as if you were treading on a sharp-edged knife—so sharp that it will seem you are bleeding. If you can bear all this, I will help you."

"Yes," said the little mermaid in a quivering voice, as she thought of the Prince and the immortal soul.

"But remember," the witch continued, "once you have taken a human shape, you can never become a mermaid again. You can never return to your sisters and your father's palace. If you do not win the love of the Prince, if he doesn't forget his father and mother for your sake and cling to you with heart and soul, letting a priest join your hands as man and wife, then you will not win an immortal soul. On the morning after he has married somebody else, your heart will break and you will become foam on the sea."

"I am willing," said the little mermaid, turning as pale as death itself.

"You will also have to pay me," said the witch, "and it is not little that I ask. You have the most beautiful voice of anyone here in the depths of the sea. You think you will be able to charm the Prince with it, but you must give that voice to me. I want the best thing you have as an exchange, because I must give you my own blood to make the potion as sharp as a two-edged sword!"

"But if you take my voice, what will I have left?" cried the little mermaid.

"Your beautiful form," said the witch, "your gliding motion, and your eloquent eyes. That is enough to beguile a human heart."

"So be it," said the little mermaid with a trembling voice. The witch set her caldron on the fire to brew the magic draught. She cut her chest

and let her black blood drop into the potion. Again and again she threw herbs into the caldron. As the potion started to bubble, it sounded like a child crying. The steam formed such strange shapes that the little mermaid became frightened.

At last the potion was ready. It looked as clear as the clearest water. "Here you are," said the witch, and she took the tongue of the little mermaid.

Now that she was mute, the mermaid swam through the underwater forest with its terrible polyps. The shining potion gleamed in her hand like a twinkling star. But all the creatures shrank back in terror when they saw it, and she passed quickly through the forest, the swamp, and the roaring whirlpools. She saw her father's palace, where the court ball had just ended. All the torches had been extinguished, and the windows and doors were shut for the night. Probably everybody was asleep inside. She did not have the courage to approach them, now that she was leaving forever. It seemed as if her heart would break with sorrow. She stole away and rose up through the deep blue sea.

It was not yet sunrise when the little mermaid reached the Prince's palace. She sat down on the marble steps. The moon shone brightly on the horizon. She drank the bitter, sharp potion. It felt as if a two-edged sword was cutting through her delicate body. She lost consciousness and fell over, as if dead.

When the first rays of the sun touched the mermaid, she awoke. She felt a stinging pain. But when she looked up, she saw the young Prince. He stood before her, his coal-black eyes fixed upon her. Under his gaze she lowered her eyes. Immediately, she saw that her fish's tail was gone. In its place were the prettiest pair of legs any girl could desire. She veiled herself with her long, golden hair because she felt that she was naked.

The Prince asked who she was and how she had come. But she could not answer. She could only stare at him sadly with her big, blue eyes. He took her by the hand and led her to his palace. With each step she felt as though she were treading on sharp knifes and needles. But she bore the pain gladly. Led by the Prince, she moved as lightly as a fairy. He and everybody else marveled at her graceful, gliding motion.

Clad in costly robes of silk and muslin, she became the fairest of all in the palace. But she remained mute, unable to speak nor sing. Beautiful slave girls, dressed in silk and gold, sang for the Prince and his royal parents. One of them sang more delightfully than any

of the others, and the Prince clapped his hands and smiled at her. This saddened the little mermaid because she knew she herself used to sing far more beautifully at her father's palace. She thought, Oh, if he only knew that I gave away my voice forever to be with him.

When the slave girls danced to the melodious music, the little mermaid lifted her arms and, rising on the tips of her toes, glided across the shining marble floor. She danced as no one there had ever danced before. As she danced, her eyes spoke more deeply to the heart than had any of the slave girls' songs. Everyone was enchanted, especially the Prince, who called her his own dear, little foundling.

She danced again and again, even though every time her foot touched the ground it seemed to her that she was treading on sharp knifes. The Prince declared that she must always stay with him. She would, he said, be permitted to sleep on a velvet cushion outside his door. He even had a man's dress made for her, so that she could accompany him on horseback. Together, they rode through green woods and fragrant meadows. She picked flowers and listened to the birds sing. As they climbed the snow-capped mountains, her delicate feet bled so much that even the others noticed. But she only laughed and followed her Prince until they were so high that they could see the clouds moving far below, like flocks of birds on their way to distant lands.

One night, her sisters appeared, singing mournful songs as they swam by. When she waved to them, they recognized her. They swam closer and told her how much everybody had grieved for her. After that, they visited their little sister every night. Once, in the far distance, she saw the Sea King, with his crown upon his head, and her old grandmother, who had not been above the water for many years. They stretched out their hands toward her, but she could not hear their voices because they did

not dare come as near to the shore as did her sisters.

Day by day she grew dearer to the Prince. He loved her as one loves a good child, but he had no thought of making her his Queen. Yet she must become his wife, or everything would have been in vain. Instead of winning an immortal soul, on the morning after his wedding she would become foam on the sea.

"Am I not dearer to you than anyone else?" her eyes seemed to ask when he took her in his arms and kissed her fair brow.

"Yes, you are dearest of all to me," said the Prince, who understood her question, "for you have the kindest heart of all. And you remind me of a young girl whom I once saw, but whom I will probably never see again. I was on board a ship that was wrecked. The waves carried me ashore near a holy temple where some young maidens were serving. The youngest found me and saved my life. I saw her but once, yet she is the only one in the world I could ever love. You look like her and you've almost taken the place of her image in my heart. Because she belongs to that holy temple, I believe destiny has sent you to me, to remind me of her. For this reason, we will never be parted."

One day, his parents urged the Prince to marry the beautiful daughter of a neighboring King. A splendid ship was brought, so he could sail to the foreign land and visit the Princess. The little mermaid shook her head and smiled, for she knew the Prince's thoughts better than anyone else did. "I must go away," he had said to her, "to see the beautiful Princess. My parents insist upon it. But they will not force me to bring her home as my bride. I cannot love her. She is not like the maiden in the temple whom you resemble. If I ever have to chose a bride, I would sooner chose you, my mute foundling with the speaking eyes!" As he kissed her red lips, played with her long hair, and laid his head on her heart, she dreamed of human happiness and an immortal soul.

"I hope you are not afraid of the sea," he said as they stood together on the ship that was carrying them to the country of the neighboring King. He told her of the storms at sea, that were always followed by calm waters. He spoke of strange fish and terrible beasts in its

depths, and about mother-of-pearl and flowers that grow beneath the surface. She smiled at his descriptions, for she knew more than anyone else about the bottom of the sea.

In the moonlit night, when everyone was asleep except the helmsman, she sat by the rail and gazed into the water. She fancied she saw her father's palace and her garden, her grandmother with a silver crown on her head, and her sisters who looked at her with sorrowful eyes. But everything vanished like foam on the sea when her fellow travelers awoke.

The next morning the ship sailed into the neighboring King's harbor. The Prince and his company were received with great honor. The town was decorated and many court balls were held in celebration. But the young Princess had not yet arrived. People said she was staying at a holy temple, where she was learning every royal accomplishment.

At last she arrived. The little mermaid waited anxiously to see her beauty. She had to admit she had never seen a more graceful form than that of the Princess. Her face was pure and clear, and behind her long, dark eyelashes smiled a pair of dark, blue eyes. "It is you," exclaimed the Prince, "who saved me when I lay like a corpse on the shore!" And he clasped his blushing bride-to-be in his arms.

"Oh, I am more than happy!" He turned toward the little mermaid. "My dearest wish, the one thing I never dared to hope for, has been granted me. You will rejoice in my happiness," he said to her, "for you are more devoted to me than anyone else."

As the little mermaid kissed his hand, her heart was breaking. His happiness would bring her death and change her to foam on the sea.

His betrothal was celebrated and people everywhere rejoiced. On every altar fragrant oil burned in silver lamps. The priests swung their censers as the bride and bridegroom joined hands and received the blessing of the High Priest. Clad in gold and silver, the little mermaid held the bride's train. But her ears heard nothing of the festive music, her eyes saw nothing of the holy ceremony. Her mind was on the last night she had to live and all she had lost in this world.

That evening, the bride and bridegroom boarded the ship. Again, red and green fires were burning, cannons were fired, and flags waved in the air. In the middle of the ship, a big gold and purple tent had been furnished with the most beautiful curtains and cushions. Here the bridal couple were to sleep in the calm, cool night. The

sails swelled out in the breeze, and the ship glided smoothly over the calm waters.

When it grew dark, colored lanterns were lit. Music and dancing filled each room. The little mermaid remembered the first time she had risen to the surface of the sea and seen such splendor and joy. Despite her pain, she joined in the festivities. She danced as she had never danced before. And everybody adored her. Her delicate feet seemed to be cut by sharp knifes, but she could not feel it, so great was the anguish in her heart.

She knew this was the last evening she would ever see the Prince, for whom she had forsaken her home, given away her beautiful voice, and suffered untold agony. And all of this while he remained unaware. It was the last night during which she would breathe the same air as he; the last night she would see the deep ocean and the clear, starry sky. An eternal night awaited her, without thoughts or dreams, without an immortal soul—or even the chance to win one.

The merriment lasted until long past midnight as the little mermaid laughed and danced with the thought of death in her heart. She watched when the Prince kissed his beautiful bride, played with her long, dark hair, and finally left arm-in-arm with her to rest in their splendid tent.

Silence fell upon the ship. The helmsman stood at the wheel and steered the ship according to the stars. The little mermaid laid her arms on the railing and gazed toward the east to wait for the dawn. She knew that the first rays of the sun would kill her.

Then she saw her sisters rising out of the sea. They were pale and their beautiful, long hair no longer fluttered in the wind—it had been cut off!

"We have given our hair to the witch," they cried, "so that we may save you from dying tonight! She has given us a knife. Do you see how sharp it is? Before the sun rises you must plunge it into the Prince's heart. When his warm blood splashes over your feet, they will change into a fish's tail. You will become a mermaid again. You will be able to return with us and live three hundred years before you turn into dead, salty foam on the sea. Make haste! Either he or you must die before the sun rises. Kill the Prince and return to us. Do you see that red streak in the sky? In a few minutes the sun will rise and you must die!" They uttered a deep sigh and disappeared in the waves.

The little mermaid went to the tent. She drew back the purple curtain. The beautiful bride lay sleeping with her head on the Prince's breast. The mermaid bent down and kissed his fair

brow. Then she looked up at the sky where the first rays of sun were touching the clouds. She looked at the sharp knife, and again fixed her eyes on the Prince's face. In his sleep he was murmuring the name of his bride. She, and only she, was in his thoughts and in his heart.

The knife quivered in the little mermaid's hand. But her love was stronger than her pain and disappointment. For the second time she aved the Prince's life. She ung the knife far out into the waves! They gleamed red when it fell, as though spraying blood from an open wound. Once more, full of melancholy, she looked at the Prince. Then she threw herself from the ship. And her body dissolved into foam.

The morning sun rose over the sea. Its warm rays fell upon the cold foam. But the little mermaid did not feel her death. She saw the bright sun and, floating above her, hundreds of beautiful, ethereal beings. They were so transparent that she could see the white sails of the ship and the rosy clouds through them. Their voices were music, such unearthly music that no human ear could hear it, just as no human eye could see their forms. The little mermaid saw that she, too, had a body like theirs, and that it was freeing itself more and more from the foam. She turned her eyes toward the sun and for the first time felt the relief of tears in her eyes.

Suddenly, there was noise and bustle on the ship. People ran back and forth. The little mermaid saw the Prince and his young bride searching for her. With sorrow they gazed at the bubbling foam on the sea, as if they knew she had thrown herself into the waves. The mermaid floated to the ship, kissed the bride on her forehead and once again touched the Prince's face with her hand. Then, on the rays of the sun, she rose to heaven to join the other souls.

From now on, this would be her home. Through her transformation into a human being, through her sorrow and her sacrifice, the little mermaid had won a soul that could enter the higher worlds. She had reached the goal of all her longing, and found true and lasting fulfillment.

The Sacrifice

Epilog to the fairy tale The Little Mermaid

The Little Mermaid is one of the many timeless fairy tales told by Hans Christian Andersen. Its wisdom still touches the people of today's world and fills them with deep happiness.

But Andersen's fairy tales are not simple fairy tales. This writer with a "lonely heart" retreated from a loveless life into the world he created through his stories. Unable to find love despite many sacrifices, he came to believe in a love greater than human reason. He believed in the immortality of the human soul, in a life beyond good and evil, and in the surrender of all sorrow through the greater power of goodness. All his stories and fairy tales are reflections of his life and his spiritual realizations.

The paintings that Sulamith Wülfing created for this book reflect, in line and color, the essence of the story of the little mermaid's love, for which she sacrificed everything, even her own love for the Prince. A new translation was used for this book, one that strongly reveals the aspect of sacrifice inherent in the story. For this reason, parts of the story have been summarized without, in our opinion, detracting from its form or spiritual meaning.

Otto Schulze*
Elberfeld, Christmas 1953

*Otto Schulze is Sulamith Wülfing's son.

Sulamith Wülfing, Self Portrait 1953

Sulamith Wülfing
A Brief History of Her Life

Sulamith Wülfing was born in 1901 in Wuppertal-Elberfeld, Germany. Despite the protestant denomination of her parents, she was given the beautiful Jewish name Sulamith.

After finishing her high-school education, she attended art academy for four years. And when only twenty-two years old, she had her first exhibition in her home-town, Wuppertal.

In 1929, she and her husband, Otto Schulze, a Professor at the art academy in Wuppertal, founded a publishing house, where her husband was president until his death in 1976.

In 1933, their first son was born and died on the same day. Three years later, they had a second son, Otto, who eventually became Sulamith Wülfing's life-long helper in her work.

In the Second World War, she was persecuted by the Nazis and had to flee with her son and mother while her husband fought for Germany. During the war, the family experienced a number of tragic events, before they eventually met again at Christmas 1945. Sulamith Wülfing has always been convinced that only the spiritual support of Jiddu Krishnamurti, whom she honored as her teacher, prevented her from being transferred to a concentration camp by Hitler's SS.

For Sulamith, the years after the Second World War were filled with intense artistic activity and publishing. She died in March 1989 at the age of 88.

She is an internationally acclaimed artist and critics called her "Dürer's Little Daughter." But more than anything else, her art touched the hearts of countless people throughout the world.

* The photo shows Sulamith Wülfing in 1928.

Sulamith Wülfing
A Brief History of Her Life

Sulamith Wülfing was born in 1901 in Wuppertal-Elberfeld, Germany. Despite the protestant denomination of her parents, she was given the beautiful Jewish name Sulamith.

After finishing her high-school education, she attended art academy for four years. And when only twenty-two years old, she had her first exhibition in her home-town, Wuppertal.

In 1929, she and her husband, Otto Schulze, a Professor at the art academy in Wuppertal, founded a publishing house, where her husband was president until his death in 1976.

In 1933, their first son was born and died on the same day. Three years later, they had a second son, Otto, who eventually became Sulamith Wülfing's life-long helper in her work.

In the Second World War, she was persecuted by the Nazis and had to flee with her son and mother while her husband fought for Germany. During the war, the family experienced a number of tragic events, before they eventually met again at Christmas 1945. Sulamith Wülfing has always been convinced that only the spiritual support of Jiddu Krishnamurti, whom she honored as her teacher, prevented her from being transferred to a concentration camp by Hitler's SS.

For Sulamith, the years after the Second World War were filled with intense artistic activity and publishing. She died in March 1989 at the age of 88.

She is an internationally acclaimed artist and critics called her "Dürer's Little Daughter." But more than anything else, her art touched the hearts of countless people throughout the world.

* The photo shows Sulamith Wülfing in 1928.